THE MIDNIGHT OWL

Lily the Elf

For my own granny, Sylvia, who inspired bravery in me. AB

For Es and all the little ones in my life. LC

First published in 2015
by Walker Books Australia Pty Ltd
Locked Bag 22, Newtown
NSW 2042 Australia
www.walkerbooks.com.au

The moral rights of the author and illustrator have been asserted.

National Library of Australia Cataloguing-in-Publication entry:
Branford, Anna, author.
The midnight owl / Anna Branford; illustrator: Lisa Coutts.
ISBN: 978 1 925081 05 3 (paperback)
Series: Branford, Anna. Lily the elf.
For primary school age.
Subjects: Elves – Juvenile fiction.
    Fairies – Juvenile fiction.
    Owls – Juvenile fiction.
Other Creators/Contributors: Coutts, Lisa, illustrator.
A823.4

The illustrations for this book were created with
watercolour and pen and ink
Typeset in Bembo Educational
Printed and bound in China

WALKER BOOKS
AND SUBSIDIARIES

LONDON • BOSTON • SYDNEY • AUCKLAND

THE MIDNIGHT OWL

Lily
the Elf

Anna
Branford

Illustrated by Lisa Coutts

❀ Chapter ❀ one

Lily lives with her dad
in a tiny elf house,
hidden under a bridge
in a busy city.

In the moss garden behind the house there is an even tinier house called a granny flat. And in the granny flat lives Lily's granny.

It is midnight and Dad is snoring. But Lily is wide-awake. An owl is hooting.

Lily shivers with each hoot.

"Who's awake? Who?
Whoooo?" asks the
midnight owl.

Lily covers her ears
with her pillow.

"Who's awake? Who? Whoooo?"

Lily shivers and shivers.

In the morning, Lily, Dad and Granny have breakfast together.

"Did you hear the midnight owl last night?" Lily asks. "He kept asking the same spooky question."

"A spooky question?" says Granny. "I only heard cheery singing! *Moon! Lovely full moooon!*" (Granny does a very good owl hoot.)

"No," says Lily. "He was asking *Who's awake? Who? Whoooo?*" (Lily does a very good owl hoot too.)

"Poor owl," says Dad. "He doesn't mean to be spooky. He's a friendly old bird really."

Lily wishes she was braver. It seems mean to be scared of a friendly old bird. (Even if he does hoot spooky questions at midnight.)

After breakfast, Dad has to go and help a moth fix its cocoon.

"Lily, I have something I'd like to show you," Granny says.

Lily follows her into the flat.

Chapter two

Granny hunts in her wardrobe and finds a huge stripy feather.

Lily strokes it gently.

"It's beautiful," she says.
"Where did you get it?"
"My father
gave it to
me," says
Granny.
"And
his father
gave it
to him."
"But who
gave it to *him?*" asks Lily.

"The midnight owl," says Granny. "Long ago the smallest owlet went missing." (Lily knows that "owlet" is the proper name for a baby owl.) "The elves and owls searched and searched. But it was my grandfather who finally found her."

Lily listens.

(She likes hearing about her brave family.)

"The owl cried with happiness," says Granny. "He gave my grandfather his finest feather."

Lily picks it up and swishes it around.

"I wish *I* could find a missing owlet," she says. "But I don't think I'm brave enough. Even the

smallest owlet's hoot
would make me shiver."

"You might be less
shivery around owls if you
met one," says Granny.
"I have an idea. Let's visit
the midnight owl. It will
be an adventure!"

Lily puts the
feather down.

"No," she says.

"Remember," says Granny, "you are the great-great-granddaughter of an owlet-rescuer. You might be braver than you think."

"No, no, no," adds Lily (just to be clear).

Chapter three

Lily would like to go on an adventure.

So she decides to practise being brave.

She reads her scariest book.

She tiptoes around in
the dark cellar.

She even jumps off the
biggest toadstool in the
moss garden.

Slowly, she starts to feel a bit braver. "If we *did* visit the midnight owl," she asks Granny, "when would we go?"

"In the evening," says Granny. "When he wakes up."

(Lily likes staying up late.)

"Would we wear gumboots?"

"Definitely," says Granny. "It's very muddy."

(Lily has brand-new ones.)

"Would we take snacks?" asks Lily.

"We'd take a twilight picnic," says Granny, "with ginger snaps."

(Ginger snaps are Lily's favourite.)

Lily wonders what clothes a brave elf would wear. She tries on her new gumboots. Then her matching woolly hat. Then her warmest jacket. She looks in the mirror.

She does look quite brave.

"If we *did* visit the midnight owl," says Lily, "I could wear this."

"Perfect," says Granny.

Granny has been trying on clothes too. Her purple gumboots match her purple woolly hat. Both match her purple backpack. She is packing

cheese, elf pears
and ginger
snaps.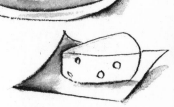

"Just in case,"
she explains.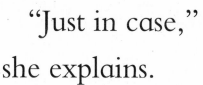

"If the owl hooted,
could we hold hands?"
asks Lily.

"Of course," says Granny.

"With my other hand, could I hold the feather?" checks Lily.

"Why not?" asks Granny.

Lily takes a deep breath.

"Granny," she says, "I think I'm feeling braver. Let's visit the midnight owl."

"Hooray!" cheers
Granny.

Chapter four

"What are you two dressed up for?" asks Dad, when he gets home.

"We're going to meet the midnight oooowl," hoots Lily.

"I thought he scared you," says Dad.

"I'm the great-great-granddaughter of an owlet-rescuer," says Lily. "I might be braver than I think."

Soon, it is time to go.

"We'll be back before

midnight," promises
Granny.

Lily follows Granny
along a steep path, up to
the bridge.

The roar of traffic gets closer. Suddenly, they pop through a crack in the concrete. Giant cars and buses whoosh past.

Next they cross the bridge.

"Will the humans see us?" asks Lily.

"They're all too busy hurrying home," says Granny.

The path curves down
into the long grass.
Granny lights her lantern
and they lay out their
twilight picnic.

(Ginger snaps are even nicer at a twilight picnic, Lily thinks.)

As they pack up, they hear a long hoot. Lily shivers.

"Good, he's awake!" says Granny. "Now we'll find him easily."

They follow the hooting sound. At last they reach the great oak tree.

"Who are you? Who, whoooo?" hoots the owl.

"I'm the granddaughter of the elf who saved your owlet!" Granny shouts. "And I have my own granddaughter with me!"

Lily trembles. But she waves the feather.

"Is it true? Ooh! Ooooh!" hoots the owl.

In a noisy fluster, he lands beside them. Lily squeezes Granny's hand. The owl peers closely at the feather. "It's you! It's truly yooooou!"

Lily covers her ears and hides behind Granny.

Granny giggles.

Chapter five

Granny and the owl chat
and hoot like old friends.
Lily watches the owl
closely.

His beak is sharp. But
Dad might be right. His
eyes look almost friendly.

The owl invites them to see his nest. He says he can fly them up on his back.

Lily squeezes Granny's hand tightly.

Lily takes a deep breath. She lets the owl help her onto his back with Granny.

It is a bumpy ride. But it is worth it.

From the owl's nest,
they can see the whole
city starting to twinkle.
He tells them funny
stories about his owlets,

and their owlets, and their owlets.

"Can I ask you something?" says Lily.

"Please doooo," hoots the owl.

"What were you saying at midnight last night?"

The owl thinks. "Well, last night I was lonely, so first I asked if anyone was awake," he says.

"Then I saw the moon,
so I sang it a song."

Lily and Granny smile.

"Oh!" says Granny
suddenly. "I promised
your dad we'd be back by
midnight! We'll be late!"

"I'll fly you home," says the owl. Lily doesn't shiver very much. She is the great-great-granddaughter of an owlet-rescuer. (She is much braver than she thinks.)

That night in bed, Lily
listens to the owl hooting.
"Soooooooooon,
little elves! Come back
soooooooon!"

Lily does not shiver
at all.

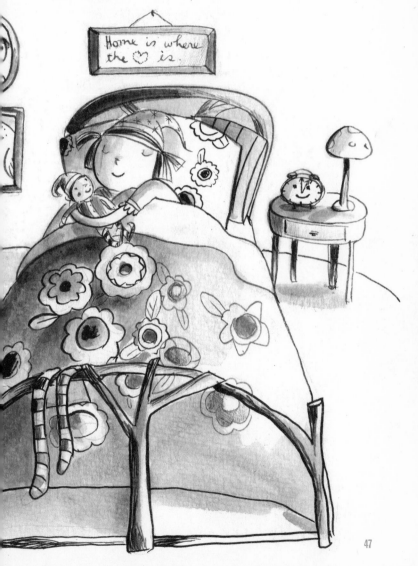

Home is where
the ♡ is.

Other
Lily the Elf
books by

Anna Branford

Lily the elf finds a
beautiful ring.
9781925081046

Dandelion seed wishes
always come true –
don't they?
9781925081060

Lily the elf has a
brand-new elf flute.
9781925081077